The Bird

By Carmel Reilly

Illustrations by Judy Spittle

Chapter 1

Max Pounces

It was late in the afternoon and Gemma sat outside watching her cat, Max.

She could see him crouching low in the grass and she wondered what he was doing. Gemma was just about to call out to Max when she saw him creeping swiftly and silently across the lawn.

Suddenly, he leapt into the air and pounced on a small bird that had just landed nearby.

"Oh no!" Gemma cried out. "Max! Let that bird go!"

Max clutched the bird between his teeth and began to run towards the back fence. Gemma jumped up and followed him.

"You put that bird down, Max!" she yelled.

Just as Max reached the end of the garden, he dropped the bird and leapt up onto the fence. He sat on the top looking down grumpily at Gemma.

"Max," said Gemma, as she ran to where the bird lay. "Oh, what have you done?"

The little bird lay very still on the grass. At first Gemma thought it was dead, but when she looked closely at it she could see its chest rising and falling in small jerky movements.

As Gemma gently picked the bird up, she saw that it was still very young – not much bigger than a chick. "I'm going to look after you, little one," she said, as she carried it inside.

Chapter 2

Making a Nest

Gemma's dad was in the kitchen.

"Look, Dad," said Gemma. "Max tried to grab this bird in the garden, but I saved it."

Dad walked to the bench to have a closer look. "Oh dear, that bird doesn't look very well. It's had a terrible shock," he said.

Gemma looked straight at her father. "I'm going to look after it and make sure it's all right. What should I do?" she asked.

Gemma's dad went to the hall cupboard and found an old cardboard box and a soft towel. He spread the towel across the bottom of the box and made a little nest.

"You can put the bird in here. It needs to be kept in a warm, dark place and left to rest," he told Gemma.

Gemma put the bird carefully in the nest, pulled the towel up close around it, and then loosely covered the box with a cloth to block out the light.

When Gemma's mum came home from work, she suggested that Gemma could feed the bird some soft cooked oatmeal and give it some water to drink.

Gently, Gemma placed two small bowls in the box in front of the bird. The bird looked nervously at Gemma, but it didn't move.

Chapter 3

A Surprise in the Night

When bedtime came, Gemma carefully carried the box into her bedroom. She put the box on top of her drawers, close to her bed.

She turned off the light and listened to the silence. "Little bird," she whispered. "Please get better."

As she drifted off to sleep, she thought she could hear a soft chirping sound. But she also felt that something was wrong.

Sometime later, she woke with a start. She heard a loud thud and then soft padding noises. At first she didn't know what the noises could be. She thought she must be dreaming. But then she heard the padding sounds again, and suddenly she realised what they were – Max's footsteps.

"Max!" she yelled. She sat up, leaned over and turned on the light just in time to see Max's tail disappear around the corner of the bedroom door.

A moment later, hearing Gemma's call, her dad appeared. He saw Gemma bending over the box crying.

"Oh no, what's happened?" he asked.

"I left the door open," sobbed Gemma. "And Max came in."

Gemma's dad looked into the box, expecting the worst. He was surprised to see the little bird staring up at him.

"Well, at least the bird seems all right. It was lucky you woke up when you did and scared Max away, but I think we'd better close your bedroom door this time."

Gemma lay awake for what seemed like hours to her. The bird was so quiet now that she began to worry, but her dad had told her not to turn the light on again. He said the bird needed to rest.

Just as she was finally falling asleep, she thought she heard the sound of feathers rustling against the cardboard.

Chapter 4

Say Goodbye

In the morning, Gemma woke to see her mum peeping under the cloth on top of the box. Mum was looking very happy.

"I think the bird is well enough to let go now," she said.

"Let go?" said Gemma. "But can't I keep it?"

"I'm sure Max would like that," said her mum laughing. "Besides, this bird is wild and it needs to be outside. We have to set it free."

Gemma, Mum and Dad carried the box out into the backyard and gently tipped it onto its side.

Gemma watched as the bird hopped to the edge, and stood for a moment preparing itself to fly. Trembling slightly, it stretched its wings and lifted off the ground, a little wobbly at first. It flew into a nearby tree and then, after a few minutes, it flew on to another tree before finally disappearing into the distance.